Enid Blyton

A FARAWAY TREE
ADVENTURE

The Land of Magic
MEDICINES

For Verity
A. P.

Text first published in Great Britain as chapters 20-22 of *The Magic Faraway Tree* in 1943
First published as *A Faraway Tree Adventure: The Land of Magic Medicines* in 2016
by Egmont UK Limited
This edition published in 2021 by Hodder & Stoughton Limited

1 3 5 7 9 10 8 6 4 2

The Magic Faraway Tree ®, Enid Blyton ® and Enid Blyton's
signature are registered trade marks of Hodder & Stoughton Limited
Text © Hodder & Stoughton Limited
Cover and interior illustrations by Alex Paterson © Hodder & Stoughton Limited

LONDON BOROUGH OF
RICHMOND UPON THAMES
DISCARDED

90710 000 456 907

Askews & Holts 20-Jan-2021

JF
LIBRARY SERVICE

RTHAW

ISBN 978 1 444 95985 7

Printed and bound in China

The paper and board used in this book are made from wood from responsible sources.

MIX
Paper from
responsible sources
FSC® C104740

Hodder Children's Books
An imprint of
Hachette Children's Group
Part of Hodder & Stoughton
Carmelite House
50 Victoria Embankment
London EC4Y 0DZ

An Hachette UK Company
www.hachette.co.uk
www.hachettechildrens.co.uk

Enid Blyton

A FARAWAY TREE
ADVENTURE

The Land of Magic
MEDICINES

HODDER

The World of the
FARAWAY TREE

MOON-FACE lives at the very top. In his house is the start of the **SLIPPERY-SLIP**, a huge slide that curves all the way down inside the trunk of the tree.

SILKY lives below Moon-Face. She is the prettiest little fairy you ever did see.

SAUCEPAN MAN is a funny old thing. His saucepans make lots of noise when they jangle together, so he can't hear very well.

CHAPTER ONE

The Children Are Worried

Lately the children had not had any time to visit their **friends in the Faraway Tree.** Their mother was in bed ill, and the doctor came each day.

'Just let her lie in bed and **keep her warm,**' he said to the children and their father. 'Give her what she likes to eat, and don't let her worry about anything.'

The children and Father were upset, but Father had to go out to work as usual.

2

They all loved Mother, and it was strange to see her lying in bed.

'There's all that washing that I had to do for Mrs Jones,' she said. 'No, you children are not to try and do it. It's too much for you.'

3

Moon-Face and Silky came to visit the children one morning, and were very sorry to hear that the children's mother was ill.

'She worries about the washing,' said Beth. 'She won't let us do it. **I don't know what to do about it!'**

'Oh, we can manage that for you,' said Silky at once. 'Old Dame Washalot will do it for nothing. It's the joy of her life to **wash, wash, wash!** I believe if she's got nothing dirty to wash, she washes clean things.

4

She even washes the leaves on the Faraway Tree. Is that the basket over there? Moon-Face and I will take it up the tree now, and bring it back when it's finished.'

'Oh, thank you, Silky dear,' said Beth gratefully. 'Mother will be so pleased when I tell her. She'll stop worrying about that.'

Silky and Moon-Face went off with the basket.

They took it to Dame Washalot, and how her face **shone with joy** when she saw such a lot of washing to be done!

'**My, this is good of you!**' she said, taking out the dirty things and throwing them into her enormous wash-tub of soapy water.

6

'Now this is what I really enjoy! I'll have them all washed and ironed by tonight.'

Silky was pleased. She knew how beautifully Dame Washalot washed and ironed. She went up to Moon-Face's house to have dinner with him.

'I do wish we could help make the children's mother better,' she said. 'She is such a lovely lady, isn't she? And the children love her so much. Moon-Face, can't you possibly think of anything?'

'Well, I don't think **Toffee Shocks** would be any good, do you?' said Moon-Face. 'I've got some of those.'

'Of course not, silly,' said Silky. 'It's medicine we want – pills or something – but as nobody is ill in the Faraway Tree there's nowhere to buy them from.'

CHAPTER TWO
Dame Washalot's Good Idea

That night they went to see if Dame
Washalot had finished the washing. She
had. It was washed and beautifully ironed
and folded up in the basket, ready to be
taken away.

'**I've had a lovely time,**' said the old
dame, beaming at Silky. 'My, the water I've
poured down the tree today.'

'Yes, I've heard the Angry Pixie shouting
like anything because he got soaked at least
four times,' said Moon-Face with a grin.
'He's got plums growing on the tree just
outside his house – and each time he went

out to pick them he got soaked with your water. **You be careful he doesn't come up and shout at you.'**

'If he does I'll put him into my next tub of dirty water and empty him down the tree with it,' said Dame Washalot.

'Oooh, I wish I could see you do that,' said Silky, tying a rope to the basket of washing, so that she could let it down the tree to the bottom. 'Well, Dame Washalot, thank you very much. The person who usually does this washing is ill in bed and can't seem to get better. It's such a pity. I wish I could make her well.'

'Why, Silky, the Land of Magic Medicines is coming tomorrow,' said the old dame. 'You could get any medicine you like there, and your friend would soon get better. Why don't you visit the land and get some?'

'That's a really good idea!' said Silky happily, letting down the basket bit by bit. Moon-Face had gone to the bottom of the tree to catch it. 'I'll tell Moon-Face, and maybe he and I could go and get some medicine.'

She slipped down the tree and told Moon-Face what the old dame had said. Moon-Face put the basket of washing on his shoulder and beamed at Silky.

'That's good news for the children,' he said. **'Come on, we'll hurry and tell them.'**

The children were delighted to have the washing back so quickly, all washed and ironed.

Rick set off with it to Mrs Jones. Beth ran to tell her mother that she needn't worry any more about it.

Silky told Joe and Frannie about the Land of Magic Medicines coming the next day to the top of the Faraway Tree. They listened in surprise.

'Well, I vote we go there,' said Joe at once. 'I'd made up my mind none of us would go while Mother was ill — but if there's a chance of getting something to make her better, we'll certainly go!'

'One of us must stay behind with Mother and the rest of us will go,' Joe went on.

So it was arranged that Joe, Rick and Beth should meet at Moon-Face's house early the next morning. **Then they would go up to the strange land** and see what they could find for their mother.

Frannie was quite willing to stay with her mother, though she felt a little bit left out.

She said **'Goodbye!'** to Joe, Rick and Beth soon after breakfast the next day, and promised to wash up the breakfast things carefully, and to sit with her mother until the rest of them came back.

The three of them set off and arrived outside Moon-Face's house at the top of the tree very soon afterwards.

Moon-Face and Silky were waiting for them. 'Is old Saucepan coming?' asked Joe. **'Hi, Saucepan, do you want to come?'** shouted Moon-Face, leaning down the tree.

Saucepan was with Watzisname.

Amazingly, he heard
what Moon-Face said and
shouted back: 'Yes, I'll come.
But where to?'
'Up the **ladder!**' yelled
Moon-Face. '**Hurry!**'

18

CHAPTER THREE
Rick and the Big Green Pills

So Saucepan came with them and in a little while they all stood in the Land of Magic Medicines. It was just as peculiar as every land that came to the top of the Faraway Tree!

It didn't seem to be a land at all!

When the children had climbed up the ladder to the top, they found themselves in what looked like a **great big factory** – a place where all kinds of pills, medicines, bandages and so on were made.

Goblins and gnomes, pixies and fairies were as busy as could be, stirring great pots over **curious green fires**, pouring medicines into **shining bottles**, and counting out pills to put into **coloured boxes**.

In one corner a goblin was stirring a purple mixture in a yellow bowl. Beth looked at it. **'It's a kind of ointment,'** she said to the others. **'I wonder what it's for.'**

21

'It's to make bad legs strong again,' said the goblin, stirring hard. **'Do you want some?'**

'Well, I don't know anyone with bad legs,' said Beth. 'Thank you all the same. If I did I'd love to have some, because it would be marvellous to make somebody's bad legs better.'

A pixie nearby was pouring some sparkling green medicine into **bottles shaped like bubbles.** The children and the others watched. It made a funny singing noise as it went in.

'What's that for?' asked Joe.

'Whoever takes this will always have shining eyes,' said the pixie. 'Shining, smiling eyes are the loveliest eyes in the world. Is it this medicine you have come for?'

'Well, no, not exactly,' said Joe. **'I'd like to have some, though.'**

'Oh, your eyes are smiley eyes,' said the pixie, looking at him. 'This is for sad people, whose eyes have become dull. Come to me when you are an old man and your eyes cannot see very well. I will give you plenty then.'

'Oh,' said Joe. 'Well, I won't be here then! **I've only just come on a short visit!'**

Rick called to the others. **'Look!'** he cried.
'Here's some really marvellous pills!
Watch them being made!'

Everyone watched. It was most astonishing to see.

First of all the pills were **enormous** – as large as footballs. A goblin blew on them with a pair of bellows out of which came green smoke, and they at once went down to the size of a cricket ball.

24

He then splashed them with what looked
like moonlight from a watering can. They
went **as small as marbles.**

Then he blew on them gently — and
they went as small as green peas, and
each one jumped into a pill-box with a
ping-ping-ping till the box was full.

PING! PING!

25

'**What are they for?**' asked Rick.

'To make short people tall,' said the goblin.
'Some people hate being short. Well, these pills
are made of **big** things – the shadow of a
mountain – the height of a tree – the **crash**
of a thunderstorm – things like that – and
they have the power to make anything or
anyone grow.'

'**Could I have some?**' asked Rick eagerly.

'**Take a boxful,**' said the goblin.

Rick took it. He read what was written on
the lid.

**'GROWING PILLS. ONE TO BE TAKEN
THREE TIMES A DAY.'**

Now Rick was not very tall for his age and
he had always wanted to be big. He looked
longingly at the pills. If he took three at once,
maybe he would grow taller. **That would be
great!**

He popped three of the pills
into his mouth. He sucked
them. They tasted so
horrible that he swallowed
them all in a hurry!

27

And goodness, **WHAT** a surprise when the others turned to speak to Rick. He was taller than their father! **He was as tall as the ceiling in their cottage!**

He towered above them, looking down on them in alarm, for he hadn't expected to grow quite so much, or quite so quickly!

'**Rick!** You've been taking those Growing Pills!' cried Joe. 'Just the sort of stupid thing you would do! **You're enormous!** How in the world do you think you'll ever get down the hole in the cloud?'

'Oh, do something to help me!' begged Rick, who really was frightened to be so enormous. Everyone else looked so small. 'Joe, Moon-Face – **what can I do?** I'm still growing! I'll burst out of the roof in a minutc!'

The goblins and
pixies around suddenly
noticed how fast Rick
was growing. They began to
shout and squeal.

'**He'll break through the
roof!** He'll bring it down on
top of us! **Quick, stop him
growing!**'

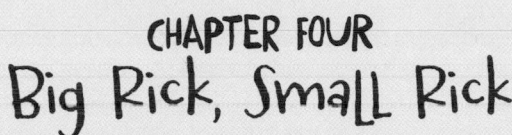

CHAPTER FOUR
Big Rick, Small Rick

Rick was **enormously tall.** He had to bend down so that his head wouldn't touch the roof. The little people in the medicine factory rushed about, yelling and shouting.

'**Fetch a ladder!** Climb up it and give him some Go-Away Pills! **Quick, quick!'**

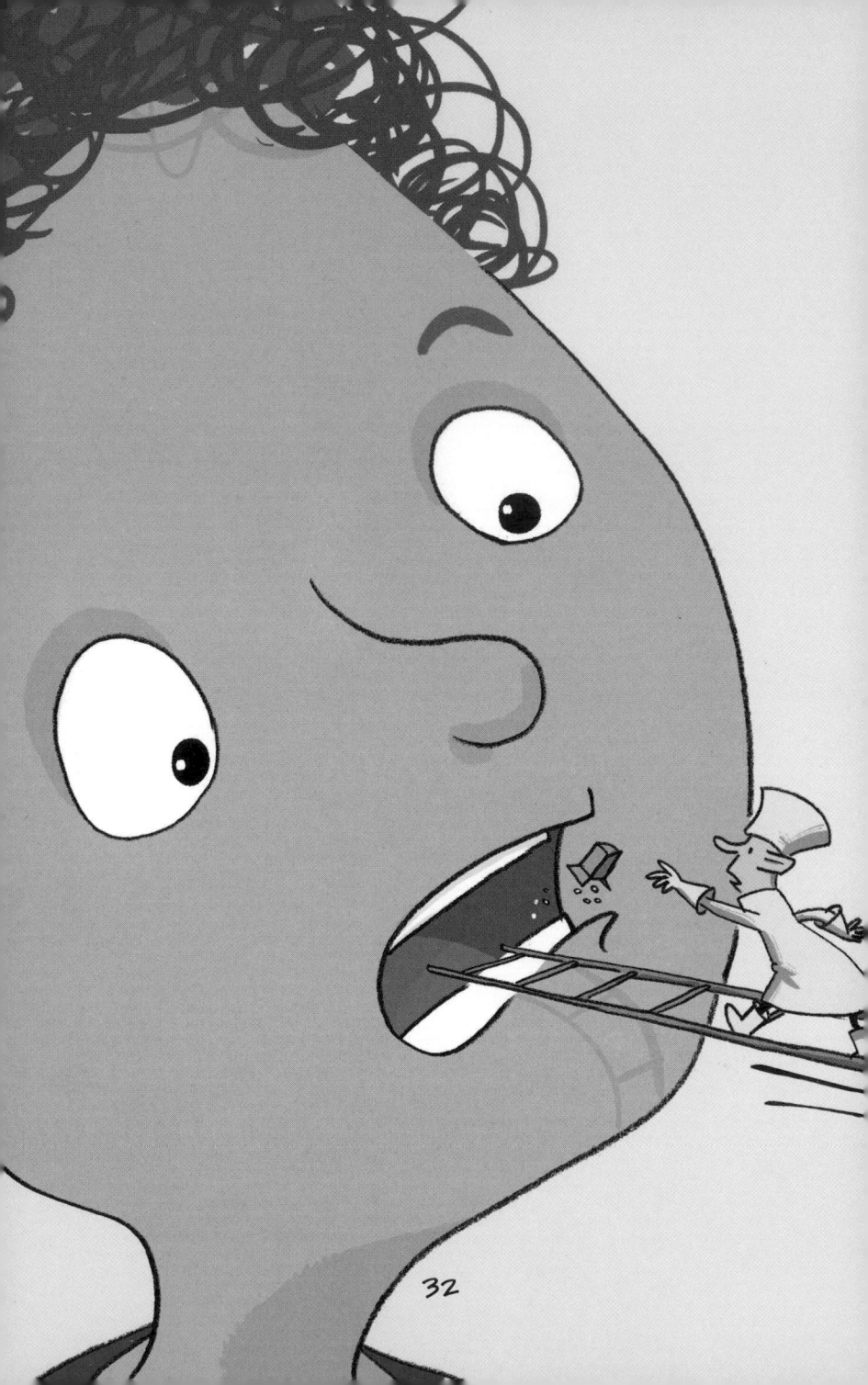

32

Somebody got a ladder and leaned it up against poor Rick.

A pixie ran up it on light feet. He carried a box of pills. He shouted to Rick: **'Open your mouth!'**

Rick opened his mouth. The pixie meant to throw one pill inside, but in his excitement he threw the whole box. **Rick swallowed it!**

And at once he began to grow small again! **Down he went** and **down** and **down.** He got to his own size and grinned with delight.

But he didn't stop there. He went **smaller** and **smaller** and smaller – and at last he couldn't be seen! It was a **terrible shock** to everyone.

'**He's gone!**' said Beth in horror. 'He's
so small that he can't be seen! **Rick! Rick!
Where are you?**'

A tiny squeak
answered her from
under a big chair.
Beth bent down
and looked there. She
couldn't see a thing.

'**Listen, Rick,**' she said. 'I've got a pill bottle here. Come running over to me and put yourself in it. Then we shall at least know where you are, even if we can't see you. And maybe we can get you right if only we've got you safely somewhere.'

A tiny **squeaking sound** came from the pill bottle after a minute, so Beth knew that Rick had done as he had been told and got into the bottle. **But she couldn't see anyone there at all.** She put on the lid, afraid that Rick might fall out.

She stood up and stared round at the wondering little folk there. **'What can we do for someone gone** too small?' she asked. 'Haven't you any medicine for that?'

'It will have to be very specially made,' said a pixie.

'We can't give him the **Grow-Fast Mixture** because he's really too small for that. We'll have to prepare a **special little bath** of powerful medicine, and get him to go into it. Then maybe he will grow back to his own size. But he shouldn't have meddled

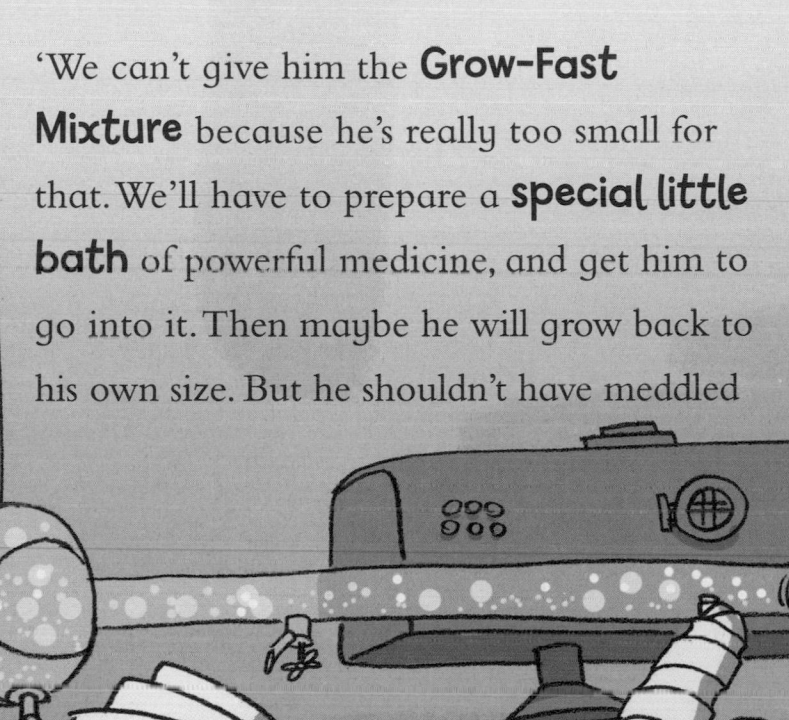

41

with our magic medicine. It's dangerous.'

'Rick's so silly,' said Joe. 'He always seems to get himself and other people into trouble! I do hope you can make him right again. I wouldn't want him to live in a pill bottle all his life.'

'We'll do our best to get him right,' said the little folk, and they began to shout here and there, calling for the most peculiar things to make the bath for Rick.

'The **whisk** of a **mouse's tail!'** cried one.

'The **sneeze** of a **frog!'** cried another.

'**The breath of a summer wind!**' cried a third.

And as the children watched, small goblins came running with little boxes and tins.

'What **peculiar things** their medicines are made of!' said Joe. 'Well, let's leave them to it, shall we? I'd like to wander round this big factory a bit more. **Come on, Saucepan.**'

CHAPTER FIVE
The Saucepan Man's Great Mistake

Saucepan was struggling to hear because there was such a noise going on all the time. Fires were sizzling under big pots. Medicines were being poured into bottles with **gurgles** and **splashes.** Pans were being stirred with a **clatter.**

Saucepan couldn't hear a word that was said — and it was because of this that he made his **great mistake.**

He stopped by a goblin who was pouring a beautiful blue liquid into a little jar. It **shone so brightly** that it caught Saucepan's eye at once.

'**That's lovely,**' he said to the goblin. '**What's it for?**'

'**To make a nose grow,**' said the goblin.

'**To make a rose grow!**' said Saucepan in delight. 'Oh, I'd like some of that. If I had that I could make roses grow on the Faraway Tree all round Mister Watzisname's branch. He would like that!'

'I said to make a **NOSE** grow!' said the goblin.

'I heard you the first time,' said Saucepan. 'It would be lovely to be able to grow roses. Do I have to drink it?'

'Yes – if you want your nose to grow,' said the goblin, looking at Saucepan's nose.

Saucepan kept on hearing him wrong.

He felt quite certain that if he drank the beautiful medicine he would be able to make roses grow anywhere! **That would be marvellous.**

So he took a jar of the medicine and drank it all up before the goblin could stop him.

'Now I'll make the roses grow out of my kettles and pans!' said Saucepan, pleased. **'Grow, roses, grow!'**

But they didn't grow, of course. It was his poor old nose that grew! It suddenly shot out, long and pink, and Saucepan stared at it in surprise. **The others looked at him in amazement.**

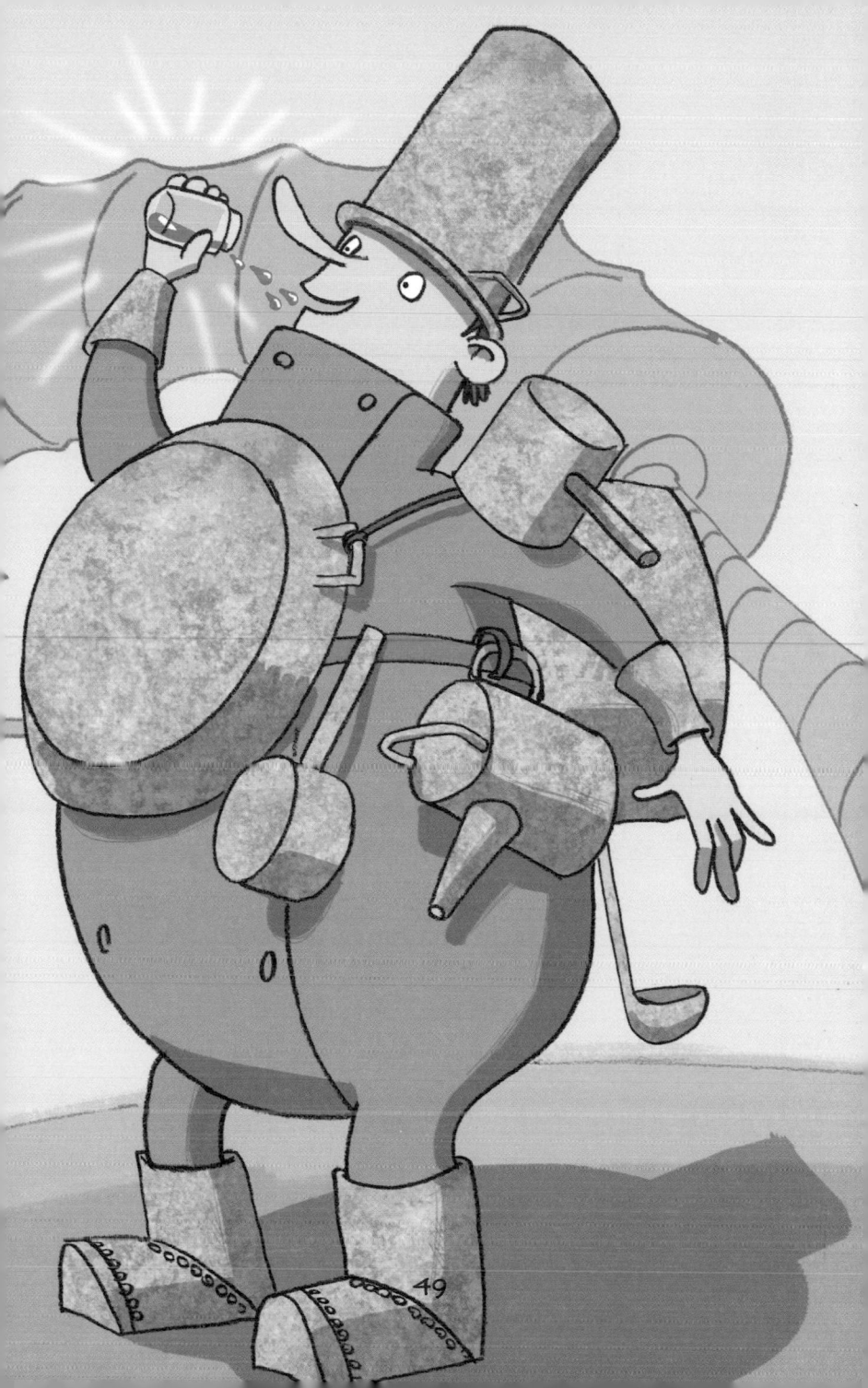

'**Saucepan! What has happened to your nose?**' cried Joe. '**It's as big as an elephant's trunk!**'

'He would drink it!' said the goblin in dismay, showing the children the empty jar. 'I told him it was to make a nose grow.

But he kept on saying it was to grow roses, not noses. **He's quite mad.'**

'No, he just couldn't hear you,' said Joe. 'Oh, poor old Saucepan! He'll have to tie his nose round his waist soon. It's down to his feet already!'

'I can cure it,' said the goblin with a grin.

'**I've got a disappearing medicine.** I'll just rub his nose with it till it disappears back to the right size. I think you ought to watch him a bit; if he goes about hearing things all wrong goodness knows what may happen to him!'

Saucepan was crying tears that rolled down his funny long nose. The goblin took **a box of blue ointment** and began to rub the end of Saucepan's nose with it. It disappeared as soon as the ointment touched it.

The goblin worked hard, rubbing gradually all up the long nose until there was nothing left but Saucepan's own pointed nose. Then he stopped rubbing.

'**Cheer up!**' he said. '**It's gone,** and only your own nose is left. My, you did look peculiar! I've never seen anyone drink a whole bottle of that nose medicine before!'

CHAPTER SIX

Rick's Bath

A shout came from behind the
watching children. **'Where's that
tiny boy in the pill bottle?** We've
got the bath ready for him now.'

54

Everyone rushed to where there was a tiny bath filled with steaming yellow water that smelt of cherries. Beth took the pill bottle from her pocket and opened it.

A squeaking came from the bottle at once.

Rick was still there, too small to be seen! But, thank goodness, his voice hadn't quite disappeared, or the others would never have known if he was there or not!

'Get into this bath, Rick,' said Beth. 'You will soon be all right again, then.'

There came the tiniest splash in the yellow water. It changed at once to pink. A **squeaking** came from the bath and bubbles rose to the surface.

Then suddenly the children could see Rick! At first it was a bit misty and cloudy – then gradually the mist thickened and took the shape of a very, very small boy.

'He's coming back, he's coming back!' cried Joe. **'Look, he's getting bigger!'**

As Rick grew bigger, the bath grew, too. **It was most astonishing to watch.**

Soon the bath was as big as an ordinary bath, and there stood Rick in it, his own size again, his clothes soaked with the pink water. **He grinned at them through the steam.**

'Just the same old cheerful Rick!' said Beth gladly. 'Oh, Rick, you gave us such a fright!'

'Step out of the bath, quick!' cried the pixie nearby. 'You're ready to be dried!'

Rick jumped out of the bath – just in time, too, for it suddenly folded itself up, grew a pair of wings, and disappeared out of a big window nearby!

'Dry him!' cried the pixie, and threw some strange towels to the children and Moon-Face. They seemed to be alive and were very warm.

The towels rubbed themselves all over Rick, squeezing his clothes as they rubbed, until in a few minutes he was perfectly dry. But his clothes were rather a curious pink colour.

'That can't be helped,' said the pixie. **'That always happens.'**

'Well, I suppose I look a bit funny, but I don't mind,' said Rick. **'Goodness, that was a peculiar adventure.'**

'A bit too peculiar for me!' said Joe. 'Now see you don't get into any more trouble, Rick, or I'll never bring you into any strange land again. I never knew anyone like you for doing things you shouldn't.'

CHAPTER SEVEN

Medicine for Mother

'Now, look here everyone,' said Joe, **'I vote
we try and get some medicine for Mother,**
and then we'll go. Frannie is waiting patiently
for us to go back, and I really think we'd better
go before Rick or Saucepan do anything
funny again.'

'What medicine do you want?' asked
a goblin kindly. 'What is wrong with your
mother?'

'Well, we really don't know,' said Rick. 'She
just lies in bed and looks white
and weak, and she worries
dreadfully about everything.'

'Oh, well, I should just take a bottle of **Get-Well Medicine,**' said the goblin. 'That will be just the thing.'

'It sounds fine,' said Joe.

The goblin poured a bubbling yellow liquid into a big bottle and gave it to Joe. He put it carefully into his pocket.

'Thank you,' Joe said. **'Now, come along everyone.** We're going.'

'Oh, Joe – there's a medicine here for making teeth **pearly,'** said Saucepan, pulling at Joe's arm. 'Just let me take some.'

'That's for making hair **CURLY!'** said Joe. 'You've heard wrong again. Don't try it.

Do you want curls growing down to your feet? Now take my arm and don't let go till we're safely back in the tree. If I didn't look after you, you'd have a nose like an elephant's, curly hair down to your toes, and **goodness knows what else!'**

They were not very far from the hole in the cloud, and they were soon climbing down the ladder, leaving behind them the strange Land of Magic Medicines. Joe was very careful of the bottle in his pocket.

'Now we'll go straight home,' he said. 'I'm simply longing to give dear old Mother a dose of this magic medicine. **It will be so lovely to see her looking well again** and rushing round the house as she always did!'

Frannie was delighted to see Joe, Beth and Rick back.

'Mother doesn't seem quite so well,' she said. 'She says she has such a bad headache. Did you get some medicine for her, Joe?'

'**Yes, I did,**' said Joe, showing Frannie the big bottle. 'It's a **Get-Well medicine.** Let's give Mother some now. It smells of plums, **so it should be rather nice.**'

They went into Mother's bedroom
and Joe took a glass and poured out two
teaspoonfuls of the strange medicine.
'Well, I hope it's all right, Joe dear,'
said Mother, holding out her hand for it.

'I must say it smells most delicious –
like plum pies cooking in the oven!'

It tasted simply lovely, too, Mother said.
She lay back on her pillows and smiled at
the children.

'Yes, I do believe **I feel better already!**' she said. 'My head isn't aching so badly.'

Well, that medicine was **simply marvellous.** By the time the evening came Mother was sitting up knitting. By the next morning she was eating a huge breakfast and laughing and joking with everyone. Father was very pleased.

'We'll soon have her up now!' he said.

And he was right! By the time the bottle of **Get-Well Medicine** was only half-finished, Mother was up and about again, singing merrily as she washed and ironed.

It was lovely to hear her.

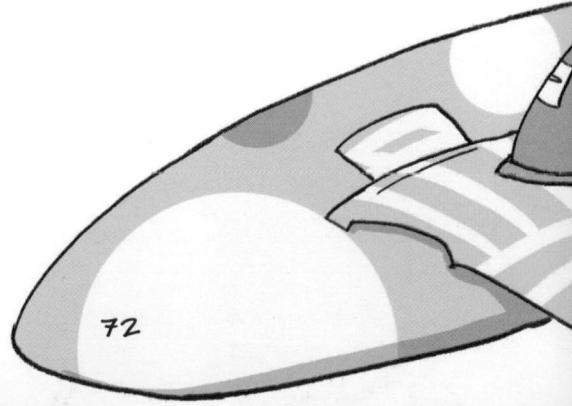

'We'll put the rest of the bottle of magic medicine away,' she said. 'I don't need it any more — but it would be very useful if anyone else is ill.'

So that's exactly what they did!